The Happy Old House

Sandi Sellen

Sandi Sellen

Illustrated by Heather Maltman Dinwoodie

The Happy Old House

Copyright © 2014 by Sandi Sellen
Illustrations by Heather Maltman Dinwoodie

ISBN: 978-1-4866-0419-7

Word Alive Press
131 Cordite Road, Winnipeg, MB R3W 1S1
www.wordalivepress.ca

WORD ALIVE
—PRESS—

Cataloguing in Publication information may be obtained from Library and Archives Canada.

Dedicated to Sandi's and Heather's Grandchildren:
Ava, Wyatt, Rhys, Paxton, Meleah, Olivia,
Emma, Lily, Micah, Maks and Ariya,
who are more precious than treasure.

"For you shall go out with joy, and be led out with peace;
The mountains and the hills shall break forth into singing before you,
and all the trees of the field shall clap their hands."

(Isaiah 55:12, NKJV)

The **Happy Old House** was built on a pretty street in a nice small town. When the house was new, it was so happy, because it had a **wonderful family**. The family had three children who loved their house.

The house had a **swimming pool** in the backyard. Sometimes the children invited friends and neighbours over. Everyone **played games** and **splashed** in the pool. Happy House loved having company and entertaining guests.

When the children were home, the house behaved the way most people's houses do. The family loved making cookies and other **delicious** things in the kitchen. Happy House loved when the family baked, but whenever the children had to go to school or church or piano lessons or gymnastics or synchronized swimming or water polo, the house did **quirky** things.

Whenever the family went out, the house **jumped** off its foundation and **ran** around town! When it saw the family driving toward home, the house would **run** fast and **jump** back on its foundation.

The house seemed to get into **mischief** when the family went anywhere. The house was full of fun and missed the children when they weren't home.

The family loved to have family nights.
They shared a TV show or a story book.

Once in a while they sang at the top of their lungs.
Almost every Friday before bed, the whole family
gathered in one of the bedrooms and
talked and laughed until late.

The house loved the stories and singing.
The walls listened carefully when secrets were told,
and it never gossiped or passed anything on in the
neighbourhood. The house loved its family, and
the family loved their house.

Precious times, like Christmas, were the happiest times of all for Happy House. The house was soooo **excited** to be able to wear beautiful decorations and lights and have a manger all set up in its family room. **Beautiful** Christmas carols echoed through the home, and friends and relatives visited and **celebrated**.

Birthdays were also wonderful, with preparations and surprises and **cakes** and **candles** and **presents** and singing. During such times, the house stayed securely on its foundation.

The children grew and grew and became teenagers. They made plans with friends to play Frisbee in the park or to go for "coffee." There would be the house **scampering** across the farmer's field so as not to miss the fun.

Oh, **tobogganing** in the winter at the hill on the edge of town was the best fun! There was Happy House jumping off its foundation again. Happy House thought no one noticed its presence, but everybody knew Happy House tagged along. It was **big** and couldn't hide very well.

The children graduated High School. It was to be a **spectacular** event. There was to be a parade in the town and a party in the evening. Of course, Happy House wanted to be there, never one to be left out and never one to miss a party if its family was there. The whole town expected to see Happy House in attendance, trying to hide its bulk.

No one had the heart to tell Happy House that its secret of jumping off its foundation and scampering around town was not a secret at all. Everyone understood that Happy House loved its family.

The town was beginning to wonder what was going to happen as the children grew older. The wonderful thing was that as the children were growing older, Happy House was growing older, too!

The children went to University. It was true that sometimes driving from University back to the small town where they lived they could still spot their house **running** quickly back to its foundation before the car drove up the driveway.

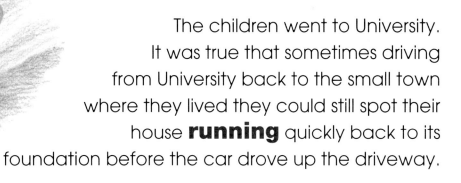

Over the years, however, the episodes of Happy House scampering all over town grew less and less. It turned out Happy Old House had collected so many wonderful memories it no longer felt the need to jump off its foundation and scurry through the town. Happy Old House remained the **liveliest** house in the town. Everyone loved Happy Old House. People would walk by just to see the house enjoying its vast collection of memories. Happy Old House smiled and laughed. Although it didn't run around town anymore, it still loved to **dance** and **sing**. That is how it came to be called The Happy **Old** House.

CPSIA information can be obtained
at www.ICGtesting.com
Printed in the USA
LVXC01n0717160314
377539LV00002B/13